Tethered

Abigail Lee Justice

Tethered

© September, 2017 by Abigail Lee Justice

Previously published December, 2016 as

Contract with a Vampire: Lucky 13, Volume One

First print edition, February, 2018

All rights reserved. No part of this book may be reproduced, scanned, or distributed in any printed or electronic form without permission. Please do not participate in or encourage piracy of copyrighted materials, this is a violation of the author's rights.

This is a work of fiction. Names, places, characters, and incidents are the product of the author's imagination and are fictitious. Any resemblance to actual persons, living or dead, events, or establishments is solely coincidental. All sexually active characters in this work are 18 years of age or older.

This book is for sale to ADULT AUDIENCES ONLY.

It contains substantial sexually explicit scenes and graphic language which may be considered offensive by some readers. Please store your files where they cannot be access by minors.

Warning the unauthorized reproduction or distributions of this copyright work is illegal. Criminal copyright infringements, including infringement without monetary gain, is investigated by the FBI and is punishable by up to 5 years in prison and a fine of $250,000.

If taboo is what you desire, take a wicked walk on the dark side.

I can give her glitz and glamour, every comfort, even make her famous, but my gifts come with a price. She must become my willing submissive. Mine to do with as I please, make her shiver or scream. But in the end, she still holds all the power, binding me with one final word...No.

One

Where does a vampire living in the underworld of Hollywood, California go for a quick meal? The answer to that question is simple. We look for the weak, the innocent or if that is not readily available, we find a hooker.

When a vampire is hungry, there is no time for the fancy shit of whining and dining. With some, I must screw with their minds first, so they only remember the incredible orgasm I gave them. Nothing more, nothing less. However, the pickings have been slim lately. I have had to use extra resources to pay a group of rowdy ex-cops to facilitate pick up and drop offs. I'm thirsty and it has been two days since I last fed. Luckily, the boys at Patches Hotel called and said they had something nice and sweet waiting for me. My mouth waters knowing that I will be feeding in under an hour.

I step out of my car and in front of me is the run-down Patches Hotel, nothing pretty or spectacular about this place. In its hay day, Patches was jumping hot with prostitutes, all the glitz and glamor associated with a brothel. Now it houses the fallen, the unwanted, and hard to handle submissives.

At least my people know how to pick from the cream of the crop. They will get me just what I want. Blade, the head overseer, meets me at the front door. He's a prick and knows it. He likes to fuck with your head if you know what I mean. I'm fortunate that he doesn't make me wait. No one makes Balton wait. Well that is not entirely true. Sometimes on the weekend, I might wait up to an hour until my room is ready.

Today he is running on time, no backups at all. As soon as I step into the front room, my nose instantly picks up the scent of a she-wolf. Pure and sweet. The scent is almost too much for me to bear. As I turn and glimpse her for the first time, I see she is thin, frail, exhausted, but her blood instantly calls me. Drinking from a she-wolf is so much better than drinking from a human.

For she-wolves, the price is steep for there are few left to feed upon, but as the ole saying goes "*you get what you pay for.*" Patches Hotel is lucky; they have thirteen she-wolves enslaved here. I know if I want this one, Blade is going to make me pay a few hundred bucks more than what I'd pay for a nasty human. Somehow he always comes out on top when dealing with his merchandise.

Could I convince her to give herself to me freely? Most she-wolves are very Alpha in nature. By the looks of this one, she could probable rip my balls off with her bare hands.

I look at Blade and say. "She'll do."

"I don't think she's your type, Balton. Why don't you stick with the human blood for now?"

I hate fucking haggling with this creep. He knows he has me by the balls, but when I want something, I will do everything within my power to get it. Or in this case, get her.

She looks directly at me. I test the waters by peering into her thoughts, she knows I am a vampire and is instantly intrigued. I can tell by the scent she emits. Pure fucking she-wolf.

"The thing about this one, doll, he plays rough. I don't want to see you get hurt," Blade said to her in a harsh tone.

"That's for damn sure," Blade isn't wrong; I love to play as hard as I can, getting everything out of my playthings. I would give anything to taste the blood of the she-wolf standing in front of me. I would even consider going a little easy on her. "If she is willing to give it a try, you know I will stay within the confines of Safe, Sane and Consensual rules of BDSM."

She looks to Blade for confirmation.

"He has no reason to lie. He plays rough but if you're willing to give him a go, I'll make sure you're paid nicely."

You need to be careful. I got no problems feeding you, and I know how to give you more.

She knew I was in her head, because she shot me an image of a vampire teaching her how to give him her aura as he fed. Just that visual had my cock hard. Without any words, she nodded to Blade and walked down the hall to her room. When we arrived, she swiped her card to open the door. *Room 13.*

She held it open so that I could enter first. Whoever had trained this little submissive had done a good job. I motioned for her to go inside, not because I think women should go first, but because I wanted to close the door behind us and lock it.

No way was I letting our first engagement be interrupted by nonsense. Too many damn predators lurking in the underground world.

The room was small compared to some that I had visited in the past, but it was surprisingly clean. Even to my nose.

"Why do I get the sense that you like to be in charge," she said with a smile as I closed the door to her room. I looked around, making sure that none of my enemies were near. You never know who could be lurking in the dark corner of a she-wolf's room. I hadn't lived this long by letting my guard down. And today was no exception.

She'd worn a lightweight dress out in the foyer but behind closed doors, she instantly pulled it off over her head to reveal her nude body to me.

I sat in the only chair in the room and telepathically ordered her: *Come here.*

She walked to me, straddled my lap, and rode up and down on my leathers, just barely touching her exposed pussy over my cock.

"Make it easy for me, baby. Think of the vampire who taught you to be a good submissive. Let me see who he was, what he was like. Do it now."

She rested her forehead on my shoulder, leaned her cheek against my throat, and she did just as I commanded. Images of her Master flashed in front of my eyes. I wasn't surprised to see a familiar vampire. *Darkeros.*

I watched as Darkeros took her through his front door, then listened as he taught her how to give her energy as he fed.

I was aware of what she was showing me, but I also skated through her mind and saw the things her Alpha had done to her, as well as the way Darkeros had treated her. She'd been giving men blowjobs when she was just a young thing, not having sex with any of them, until Darkeros had taken her at the ripe age of eighteen. He poached her virginity after she proved herself to him.

Most of her thoughts were pleasant but not all. Some memories showed how she was punished, made to do as Darkeros had taught her. If she failed to obey, he punished her in front of her pack members. He made an example out of her wrongdoing so that she didn't make that mistake again.

Darkeros had thoroughly used her, but he hadn't been cruel, he kept her nourished and hydrated as he practically bled her dry, time after time.

Apparently, her blood had called to him too, just as it was doing to me now.

I patted her ass and thought, *"Up."*

She leaned to the side, stood on her right leg, and swung her left off. I smiled at how eager she was to please me. She did it in the most graceful and pleasing way possible. My dick got even harder.

It was weird that my most recent companion had been male. I found him one night working the Hollywood strip when he was just a young buck. I fed him enough of my vampire blood that he didn't look a day over twenty although he was nearly a hundred years old. Not surprising, that's how vampire blood reacted to him, but as the decades wore on him I wanted him to live out the rest of his life, free, no longer held by my binds as he had been for so long. Letting him go hasn't been easy on me either. Even though he's leaving better than when he arrived at my house. I know it is time to let him go. Slowly I've pulled away these last few weeks. I know he knows what I'm doing.

That's why I'm here today to find his replacement. Yeah, I've been with males for decades but I also like me a fine pussy to feast upon. I don't think I tire of either. This brings me to what orifice I want to take first on my luscious she-wolf. Her ass, or her ripe pussy, but perhaps maybe it's her luscious wet mouth.

"Bend over the bed. Spread your legs." The inclination was to dive into her ass and listen to her beg and scream for me, but I also needed no to be harsh with her. I need her to agree to come home with me when all is said and done. I breathe in her scent as I remove my leathers and black silk shirt. I smell her lust and know she is already wet. I wouldn't need to prime this one. She is well trained.

I situate myself behind the wolf, resting my cock at the edge of her cunt. "Slide back onto me." It'd been centuries since I'd had a wolf this prime. She needed a nickname, something she'd respond to. Nothing fancy though until I get to know her.

I need to strip away the fake façade she wears. She had been manipulated, forced to do evil, torn down all her life. The idea of turning her into a wealthy socialite who could one day look down her nose at the Alpha who'd mistreated her suited my fancy. She needed to be decorated with sparkling jewels and dressed in fancy clothes. That's what I had done to Bernard. Sadly, he would be leaving me soon and she would be my new project.

My girl reminds me of a Tibetan princess, or more likely a victorious woman. Therefore, in the spirit of her past struggles, I think Zaya would suit her perfectly. I'd mold her into who I wanted her to be, and then someday when the time was right for her to move on, she'd be perfect to marry someone with political power, or one who has a superior position of power.

Respectfully, with enough training, I could even get her to help me behind the scenes without anyone ever knowing it. Better yet, I'd take her far, far away from the devastation we live in now and drink her dry until she couldn't change and heal, and I'd absorb her and her wolf's life force into me as they died.

After sifting through the she-wolf's head, I saw no evidence that even one person loved her. Not even her parents. Darkeros felt responsible for her, when she worked and trained under him, but there was no affection. Except for sex. She was his sex toy to be used however he felt it was necessary.

He treated her like property, the true slave she was. When her time was up with Darkeros she thought her life would change for the better, boy was she wrong. Her life went straight to hell. It gave her a whole slew of new problems. No fancy roof over her head, clothes were hand me downs or worse from her prey. At least at Patches she now had some of the things she once had at Darkeros' establishment. If she was willing to give of herself, she kept a roof over her head.

Slowly I pumped in and out of her wet cunt, taking a measure of her, I picked at other parts of her mind. In some ways, she had the brain of a rambunctious teenager, and in other images, she was a mature, classy lady.

I was puzzled. Why hadn't Darkeros kept this beautiful woman for his own? *I'll make sure, once I get her home, to reach out to some of my friends to get more information on her departure from Darkeros' service. Until then, I should probably make sure I'm not stepping on a landmine with Darkeros.* We've never had a friendly relationship and I don't aim to have one just because I used his slave.

She groaned and whined with each stroke of my cock. I fucked her until she was close to orgasm. Her thoughts clearly told me she was enjoying my cock and looking forward to my bite. I pulled out and slid into her ass with only the juices from her pussy to ease my entry. After a few yelps, she took everything

I gave her. I must give Darkeros credit; he'd done a good job of making her want it without totally addicting her to it. She'd been trained well.

Pleasure and pain now streamed through her veins. I stilled my hips and let my fangs extend. Resting my torso on hers, I let my teeth sink into her delicious neck. It had been two days since I last fed. My mouth watered with the first taste of her delectable blood. She was everything I thought she would be. I drank my fill before I put any numbing chemicals in her. I wanted her to feel my bite. To savor the sting if possible. I wanted her to feel pain as I sucked the life out of her, as she channeled her aura into me until I was nearly lightheaded from the rush of it.

I drank more than I intended, testing the waters just a bit, my sadistic side was in full bloom. I wanted to relish in the moment in case she didn't agree to come back to my lair of her own free will. She didn't know it yet, but my little she-wolf was coming home with me tonight.

I injected the cocktail to give her a series of orgasms before I finally lifted my mouth from her tiny neck, carefully sealing the puncture wounds with my saliva. Watching her body jerk and spasm as she orgasmed, her ass muscles squeeze my cock. Groaning in ecstasy, I released my seed deep in her ass. I pounded her without mercy until my energy was drained.

Her mouth was aimed into a pillow so that her screams of bliss were absorbed into the fabric. My girl was out of breath and limp by the time her orgasm faded. I lifted her into my arms and cradled her on my lap as she peacefully stilled.

I knew I had to have more. Showing affection to someone you don't have feelings for and yet want in your life can be tricky. I knew my feelings were purely for the sexual pleasures she could give, but I saw something else hidden deep under her façade. Even though I was paying for her body, I felt something tug on my heartstrings. Her breathing had slowed. Her eyes were still closed she was in sub space. She was a true submissive. Floating, Floating high above the clouds. I felt it in her body as she relaxed in my arms.

She snuggled up into my arms and blinked. I stroked the top of her hair away from her face. "I'd like to take you home so we can discuss turning this into a permanent arrangement."

"What do you mean by permanent arrangement? Like a standing appointment every week? I don't have to come home with you to negotiate that. We can do that here at Patches; I have a calendar all set up. I can pencil you in. No problem. If you need to cancel, you can call Blade the morning of our appointments. Just leave your bank information with Blade. I don't have a problem with seeing you regularly."

"No, I'd like to discuss making you the wolf equivalent of a human companion."

Her body tensed in my arms. She froze for a few seconds, and I smelled fear. "You won't want me, when you find out…"

"Find out what?" I gave her a moment to ponder over what she was going to say. When she didn't speak, I told her, "Let me be judge and jury. What is it I need to find out, before I can make an informed decision? Whatever you've done before is in the past. I hold nothing against you. You have a clean slate with me."

"My old Master loaned me to other vampires for sex. Sometimes I really liked what he was doing, but there were times I absolutely hated it."

"Darkeros did this to you?"

"You know him?"

"Yeah, I spent some time with him a few decades back running the streets of the underground but nothing since then. He's pretty much stayed to his side of the tracks and I've stayed on mine. You no longer belong to him; you belong to Blade now. If you'd like, I can place a phone call to Darkeros to see why you're holding back on me."

"No, that's not necessary. He wasn't all that bad, our time just was over. He found someone younger and willing to service him in other ways. I needed to use my own willpower to better myself. We came to an agreement, and I left. Darkeros wasn't looking for someone strong like me; he wanted someone to bend to his beliefs only. So, he freed me."

"Did you know I was in your head, or did you guess?"

"I felt you looking in the lobby. I didn't look to see where you explored while we were having sex, so I don't know which memories you saw, but I'm pretty sure you saw a bunch of them."

She was right I saw everything I needed to see to know that she was the one for me. I still wanted to take her home. I knew I needed to override her will, I couldn't trust her as I could a human companion, but I could mold her that way we could work together. Shower her with the things she never had at her disposal. Turn her into someone of importance.

She hid extreme powers and only used them when needed. I didn't mind that at all. I'm not the type of egotistical bastard that needed his companion to be an underling. I wanted someone at my side as my equal. I rested my hand on her cheek and opened enough to let her sense the magnitude of my power.

Her eyes grew large.

"I'm second in command to the Mordecai Realm. I've only met a few wolves I couldn't entirely control, and they were powerful Alphas who could pull on the energy of thousands of wolves. You, my dear, are just as powerful as they are but ten times more. What I'm proposing is this. Since I'm not awake during the day much, you won't have access to me during the day until I'm sure of my control, but I do believe you'll be able to live with me without physical restraints once we get it all worked out.

In the meantime, come home with me for a week. You'll be caged when I'm down. I generally wake during the afternoon, so it'll be less than ten hours and you'll likely sleep for much of it. I'll help you figure the outer limits of your abilities, and since we'll be in the trying-out stages for you to be my wolf guard, no rules will be broken."

"And if I don't want to stay at the end of the week? What then?"

"Then you'll come back here to Patches, and Blade will find you new clients."

"And if I decide to stay?"

"We'll negotiate that over the course of the week. If you're mine, you know you'll have the same rights of any first slaves of the household."

She shook her head. "No, slaves don't have any rights."

"In Mordecai's Realm, slaves have more rights than vampires. You will be treated like a princess, and if I treat you poorly, My Lord Leigh will hand you my balls on a golden platter."

I gripped her chin in my hand, forcing her to look at me. "I'm hard on my slaves. And yes, punishment can be horrible, but if you please me, know this. You will be the queen of my castle. I'll see to your every need, you'll never want, your needs will be fulfilled. I'm not saying I'm going to be easy on you, but if you disobey me, I will suck the life out of you."

The smell of fear hit my nose, but I can still hear and see her thoughts. She hasn't shut me out yet. I can tell that my words intrigue her. I've done my best to tell her exactly what I want and how I want it. It's now up to her to accept or walk away.

I enjoy the challenge of giving a slave enough willpower to get themselves in a little trouble here and there, but not enough to do serious damage. Nevertheless, this wolf intrigues me, peaks my blood to boil, bring my sadistic side out, but most of all she makes my dick harden.

My job here is done. All I must do is wait for her decision. Blade will be a hard ass, but I know he needs my money and support to keep this establishment running. It's not as if we're strangers.

We've worked before on a few projects. Nonetheless, it is not up to Blade, it's her decision.

"I'll go for a week, but if during that time, I'm not satisfied, I'm out of there. No second chances." She looked like a high-end executive at a board meeting giving the company bad news. She was stern but comfortable knowing she held the power to say NO.

****

After all the arrangements were hashed out between Blade and I, he asked to have a moment privately with Zaya. She didn't know her new name yet, but at some point, I would ease that in during the next week.

I watched as he took her into the back to talk. He thought he could stop me with his mechanical sound dampener, but I was in her head so I heard everything. Not even his walls could block me. Blade asked her questions to be sure she knew what she was agreeing to, and if she knew who I was. My little wolf was strong and held her own. It pleased me that she could stand up for herself in the manner she did. Blade was a badass but under his armor, he was just a pimp.

Two

After we gathered up her personal things, I took a good look around her room one last time. I realized she didn't have much. No fancy dresses, no expensive furniture. The only thing she cherished was a stuffed cat. As we walked out of her room, she clung to the stuffed animal for dear life.

"I know what you're thinking, Balton. Where's all my stuff? When I left Darkeros, I left everything behind. I didn't want the constant reminder where things came from."

"After dinner, I'll arrange for a seamstress to come with some fabric and make you some of the finest wares in town. As far as possessions, when the time's right we can go out and get you whatever will make you happy. You'll be surprised how generous I can be, when given the opportunity."

"I know how this works, Balton. I give you what you want and you'll give me material things." I took three steps to her and stared directly at her soul. She knew she had crossed the line, by her choice of words.

"Kneel, slave." Without hesitation, she dropped to her knees as graceful as an angel. Her eyes were full of fear and her scent permeated throughout the room. She knew I had to punish her. She had that look.

"Only my friends and worthy political associates use my first name. If I'm to own you, you may as well get used to calling me Master. No sense having a trial week without the dynamic we'll have if we take it farther."

She looked to the floor as she closed me off to her thoughts. I grinned inwardly. I hadn't expected her to have this kind of spunk, this soon. I'd let her get away with closing me out for now, but when she least expects I will remind her who her owner is.

"I'm sorry, Master. I wasn't aware I shouldn't call you by your name. I'll do better in the future. Master suites you better." She said in a low voice, never looking at me. Her eyes were glued to the small square of floor. With my hand, I lifted her dress revealing her bare ass. In one fluid motion, I slapped her right ass cheek nearly hard enough to knock her over. My graceful angel held her position with poise. I touched her cheek, felt the heat of the slap, and stroked it with my thumb. "I know you will. We'll get to know each other and everything will work out. Just remember your place, little wolf. No more testing the waters."

****

The drive back to my place had taken a little longer than I expected. My little she-wolf was starving, so I stopped at a local burger joint. She devoured every morsel. My girl had an appetite.

The entire drive home we spoke back and forth telepathically. She reminisced about her youth, her parents had left her with a pack far from their home. She never understood why her parents didn't keep her, but she knew that it was best for them. Growing up she had various jobs within the pack but nothing that expanded her gifts. Domestic housework, cleaning, and serving the pack was how she survived. When she reached sixteen, she went out on her own. For two years, she barely survived. It wasn't until Darkeros took her in that she thrived for the first time in years.

Even though he had been rough on her at times, she still craved, desired more from him. She allowed her masochistic side to take over when needed. She didn't know it, but I was going to be tough on her when we got home. Sometimes you need to break a wolf's power to bring them back to reality. And I planned to do just that. Either we'll be allied or she'll be caged.

Three

The second he closed the door to his suite of rooms, he shredded my mental walls and was back in my head. I thought I could block him, but he proved to be smarter, wiser, and craftier than I thought.

I wrapped my arms around my skull and fell to the ground with a scream, but he didn't back off and there was no way for me to push him out as he literally invaded my mind. He looked at how I had blocked him after I called him Balton. I closed him out. I'd been thinking that what he had done was just a slap on the ass, and that I had gotten worse from Darkeros. I shut him out because I'd wanted to think it through. I knew not to call him by his first name. Any beginner slave knew that was a big no, no. I wanted to push him to see how far he would go.

Apparently, I hadn't pushed far enough.

I had been able to keep everyone out so far, he would be no different from the rest. Boy was I wrong. Looked like Master Balton was ready to show me how wrong I was. He wanted me to know off the bat how strong he was. He heard me think of him by his first name, I screamed as I felt my fingers being burned. Just as I felt my skin sizzle, I realize he's just severed every thread leading back to my previous Master. He forced me to watch as he put a noose around those thoughts, sucking the memories from my mind. I couldn't do anything except scream. I couldn't block him. I felt my willpower being suppressed.

"That's it my little wolf don't fight me; I know you feel my leash. As easily as I put it on, I can take it off. It isn't permanent. *Yet.* "

All I could do was feel the leash tighten even more, my body thrashed on the floor as I continued to hold my head with my burnt fingers.

"Okay, little wolf, now you're going to orgasm for me, I want you to feel the total opposite of the pain I'm forcing into your head. I want you to be in bliss. Do it. Do it NOW. COME!"

The one thing I knew was to obey, and that's exactly what my body did, my screams were filled with pain and pleasure as tears streamed down my face. When I was done, he licked my throat on both sides. Was he preparing to bite? Just as I relaxed, I felt his teeth sink into my throat. My first instinct was to thrash about, but I learned at a very young age not to do such a thing when a Vampire had his sharp fangs buried in your neck. I had to *Trust* him.

As soon as he had his fill without removing his fangs, I heard him order me into my wolf form. As any slave, I did as I was told. As I shifted into my wolf frame, he stayed pierced to my neck. My silver shaded hair covered body took form in his arms. I felt him stroke my fur-covered body with his big masculine hands.

He drank and drank, until I thought I would have no more to give him, he knew just how much to take. Just when I was on the brink of fading out he ordered me to shift back to human form once more. The process was excruciating but I did as I was commanded. His fangs never left my neck. He liked both my human blood and my wolf blood. Just as I lost consciousness, I heard him say how pleased he was with my first challenge.

Four

I spent several hours dripping vampire blood into my little wolf's mouth after she passed out. My leash was now tethered to both her human form and her wolf's brain. She was mine. I'd force myself to release her after a week if she truly could not obey my commands. It would be hard but a promise is a promise. In the meantime, I intended to mold and craft her during this next week. *Treat her like a princess when due, shower her the fruits of the earth, but still show her who her true Master is.*

For the first time in a long time, I felt like a different person. My heart was lighter than it had been in centuries. I haven't felt this satisfied in so long. I wondered if Darkeros felt this way with her. Or did he just use and abuse her powers. Her powers were like no others I'd ever seen.

I sent a message to Mordacai to make him aware of my little she-wolf. I also felt the need to reach out to Darkeros telepathically, but he didn't respond. I didn't want him to feel like I had poached her from his lair.

Mordacai and I had a lengthy chat. I let him know what I was planning on doing with my little plaything. He graciously gave me the week off from all my duties. He felt it was time that I put my own house in order. After squaring everything with Mordacai, I checked in on my sleeping girl. She was tucked in her cage, safe and sound. My sleeping princess.

Five

Slowly I woke up from a nice long nap, to find myself locked in a cage. My wolf brain didn't like being caged like an animal. A small dish of water rested in the corner of the steel metal bars. Thirst was always a problem after having so many orgasms. Luckily, the bowl refilled continuously as I drank my fill.

Something was wrong. I tried to force my way up through the fur, I had no recollection of where I was. It took me a few minutes to see clearly. Both the wolf and my human brain were still awake at the same time. Normally this didn't happen often. I strained to remember how it felt to have fingers and toes, hips and everything a wolf had. I started to freak out. I knew that staying calm was the most important way to possible free my mind.

Normally when the human side came this far to the surface, the brain changed to human. Today, I had both wolf and human. I was mentally exhausted, but my body was in decent shape. I handled everything my Master had asked of me earlier. He fed from both of my bloods. This brain of two didn't let me reason things through as I was used to. I tried to change out of frustration but for some reason I was trapped like this.

I tried to pace in the cage but having long appendages was awkward; I'd never made this body walk before. The space wasn't much taller than I was when I walked. It hit me like a freight train that I had to pee, I was hungry, and I couldn't change. The wolf took control of this body once again. My primal instinct kicked in and came to the surface.

Instead of screaming, the wolf howled out her anger and distress. Long, thick talons scratched at the metal bar, sending a high-pitched noise throughout the room. She was full of rage.

My Master wasn't in bed. Funny how my cage was under his bed and not at the foot of the bed as it had been with Darkeros.

So as not to panic, I howled out again. As I let out the last noise, a wolf on two legs came in the room. It held a tray of fresh bloody meats. Our stomach growled we were both hungry. The wolf slid the tray through an opening in the cage. We feasted on the meats until they were gone.

Our appetite had been filled. Just like he promised. My primal needs had been met.

Six

My little Zaya had been thrashing around in the cage; I felt her frustration when I awoke. She was still in her wolf's body, and couldn't change back to her human body out of pure exhaustion. I went downstairs in a hidden room, where I'd continue to take my day's rest until I was certain I could control her even if I was asleep. Reading her mind, I knew she had feasted on the meats and had to pee. She'd sensed that I was nearing; she didn't stir or jump up when I entered the room. I bent down so that we were eye level with each other.

"Well, my she-wolf, I can see you're in control now. A wolf with human eyes is even more disconcerting than a human with wolf eyes." All she did was stare at me, she didn't move, as I had ordered her to.

It took no time at all for my wolf to change back to human form. I could tell she had no pain at all. Sometimes pain would be involved, but she seemed to handle this change unscathed. She looked recharged now that she had food and my blood in her body.

"You don't have to urinate anymore?" I asked her.

"No B," I heard her almost say but she quickly corrected herself by saying Master.

"I still want to but don't have the need to."

I read her mind and sensed she wanted to ask me to take her home, to end the experiment, but knowing that I had decided with Blade to check in at the forty-eight-hour mark. She assured me that she could at least last that long.

I helped her out of the cage and arranged her on the bed, on her back with her knees bent so her feminine parts were on full display and her arms out to her side. She didn't dare move herself; she left that to me.

"Master, was last night the worst it's likely to get?"

I held eye contact a few seconds before shaking my head. "It's impossible for me to show you how bad it can be. My little Zaya, I can be a sadistic bastard, but I will never be cruel enough to cause you harm."

"You called me Zaya. Why's that, Master?"

"I think that name suits you. I hope you like it as much as I do."

"I love it B… Master."

I can tell she's still timid about using titles around me, but getting comfortable as we talk.

"Zaya, I'd like you to use an honorific every time you speak, unless we're around humans." I didn't give her time to respond before adding, "You should have a new identity hence the new name. While you're here under my foot, I will call you Zaya as I wish or whatever other slang I choose to use. Whatever strikes my mood is how I will address you. It's your job to figure out how to respond to my will."

She opened her mouth to speak, but I held up a hand and she closed it, she was catching on quick. "As for you earlier question, if you need to be punished you'll remember every moment of your punishment. Likewise, last night was to teach you something, and thus I can't gift you with forgetfulness. However, there will be times I'll want to hurt you in ways you can't imagine, simply to hear you scream. I get off on hearing you scream, it makes me hard. If at those times, you wish not to remember, I can block your thought process to make you forget. That is in my power."

My little she-wolf was in deep thought. Her eyes blinked uncontrollably. It was the most precious thing to watch. A few seconds later, she shook her head. "Sir, I don't want to forget last night. I was wrong for calling you by your name. I'm experienced.

I should know about it. Will you promise me you won't make me forget things, Master?"

"There will be times I use my powers to make you forget. Sorry, no. If I believe, I have done something to add to your eternal misfortunes, I will wipe that memory from you. You're not strong enough to erase anything I put into your mind."

She didn't like his decision; it was written all over her face. Even her body language had changed. She knew better than to argue. Instead, she asked, "Will you promise you'll tell me when you've made me forget something? Sir."

"Unless there's a true reason I shouldn't tell you, I believe I can make that promise."

She's a smart girl. I liked that in her. It showed she was thinking on her own.

She was silent for a few moments before saying, "But you didn't make the promise, Sir. You just said you believed you could. That's not a promise."

She had me there. My choice of words played against me. She was using her Alpha skills to get what she wanted from me. That's the kind of person I want at my side. Not someone who accepts *no*. She's willing to fight for what she believes she should get.

I scratched my head, considered my options, "I'll make the promise for this week, but promises between owner and slave aren't binding unless a formal contract has been made. We only have a contract for this week. Lest not you forget that, my dear. "

I could see it in her eyes; she had won her first encounter with me. Her attitude had just done a three-hundred-and-sixty-degree turn. I dipped my hand between her folds, inserted a finger into her pussy, pulled it out, and sucked her juices clean from my finger. Sweet cream, one of my favorite desserts.

She didn't twist or turn, hell she didn't try to push me away. She liked being fingered; I slip my finger back in her pussy. Her inner walls sucked my finger like a vice grip. Yeah, my little wolf liked being finger fucked. She'd just have to wait. I had other plans for her now.

Just as fast as I pushed my finger into her pussy, I pulled it out leaving her wanting more. The look of disappointment in her eyes expressed just how she was feeling. *Disappointed.*

"I sent for the best seamstress in the underground to come with some of her finest fabrics. She even took the liberty of bringing a few of her helpers with her so that they can have any alterations done while they're here today. She should be set up downstairs. No need for you to dress in any of your things, as you'd just have to take them off." I instantly saw her cover up her neither regions.

I grabbed her arm from her pussy and said, "Never in my presence will you hide such beauty. I own that body, if I want you to parade around naked for my pleasure you will obey. Clothes are only to be used when I have meetings and you're at my side. Nothing more. Do I make myself clear?"

Hesitation was written all over her face just as I thought it would be. In time, she would be comfortable with her body. She would need to *Trust* me.

****

The walk through the huge mansion was humiliating without my clothes. I knew this would be hard but since coming yesterday I had not met any of the staff or even taken a tour of the mansion, I had only been fed by another she-wolf and fucked by my Master.

Even at Darkeros' house, I was given the choice of when and what I wanted to wear around the staff. Since this was only for one week, I knew I could handle the stress of being looked at by others. I would just need to go to that place in my mind where I would block out the rest of what was going on around me. *My happy place.*

Balton led the way through the mansion to where the seamstress and her staff were waiting for me. We passed by several staff members as we descended the spiral stairway. The walls were filled with painted murals of angelic like creatures singing, dancing, eating, and some were even engaged in graphic sexual delights. Not all were human figures; some were vampires, werewolves, and even a few mythical creatures.

My Master didn't say a word to me but did as we passed by human servants he gave then words of praise. They all wore clothes including Balton. I was the only one naked. They gawked but didn't acknowledge me in any way.

We entered a beautiful library filled with walls of books. Besides the books, the seamstress had the room full of clothes. I'd never seen such luxurious fabrics. Not even at Darkeros'.

Balton took a seat in a reclining leather chair as the women worked their magic on me. I'd never had such luxurious fabric draped over my skin. Just as Balton promised, he would make me into his perfect princess by clothing me with wealth. I immediately went somewhere else in my mind as the fabric covered my body.

Fancy me walking around on the arm of my new Master at one of the many balls he hosted. Hell, women in magazines probably felt the way I feel. Class and sophistication was written all over my body. No longer did I shame my bare skin.

Each thing I tried on was better than the last. Nothing inexpensive, but nothing had a price tag either. Balton watched without making a sound in the chair. I knew he liked something by the way he kept shifting in the chair.

A tall black man came in as I was trying on the last outfit. He brought in several large boxes and a fancy chair. Two hours later, my hair was a different color and was cut so I didn't recognize myself. I hadn't had this type of treatment ever. Darkeros always told me to make sure I was presentable when needed. Never had he chose how I would look or what I would wear. That was all put on my shoulders.

In a way, I felt special that Balton did this for me. It took the responsibility out of my hands. If this was part of him owning me, I didn't mind one bit. He could lavish my body with fancy new things anytime he wanted. I went from being an unattractive frumpy she-wolf to a desirable beautiful woman in less than four hours.

I stared in the mirror that was handed to me all I could see now was a gorgeous woman starring back at me. My hair looked like strands of gold shimmering from my head. Once the final touches were put on my hair, another man did my makeup. He had every color choice on a painter pallet. I was only used to using my usual purples, blues and black to make my eyes stand out. This guy though had colors I had never seen before. I didn't have these types of treats growing up. Money had been very tight. I never had nice things at all everything I had come from hand me downs or I killed to get.

Tears streamed down my face. Thinking about where I had come from and where I was now. These people had transformed me into someone else.

A true lady.

The man started to fuss at me about messing up his beautiful creation.

"Then you'll fix it for Zaya," I heard my Master say. I hadn't heard him say anything in four hours. For that matter, I hadn't heard him approach me in the fancy chair. But now he leaned on the chair. "It's just makeup; it's meant to be washed off and applied again, my dear."

His words were meant to calm me, sooth me in a way I had never had before. I felt at that moment he was showing me a side of his emotions that I hadn't seen yet. "Why are you crying?"

"I had no idea I could be... this person!" I pointed towards the mirror.

"My dear, you are seeing the real you for the first time. All I have done is pay a seamstress and stylist to show you the possibilities of what can be done with a beautiful canvas."

Balton took his handkerchief out of a pocket and dabbed at my eyes. His touch was so gentle and it was comforting knowing he had that side to him. My Master sighed and told me, "If you stay with me, you'll learn all the manners of society's elite, and someday I'll take you to a function where your old Alpha Pack serves at. They can serve you as you once did to them years ago."

"But Master, I won't have any power, I'll still be your slave."

"Yes, Zaya you'll be my slave, but you'll have all the power. Except for My Lord and me, we hold the power over you, but rest assured I'll make certain you have it over anyone else you wish within reason, of course. Our political allies will become yours as well, and you'll have to learn how to keep them on our side. You my wolf, hold the key to your heart and to your happiness. In time, you'll come to know how and why that is. For now, you need to trust me." Gently he kissed the top of my nose, sending all the unhappiness away.

"Here's a rule. From this point forward, we don't refer to Darkeros as your old Alpha. Yes, I read your mind and saw the unhappiness. I want you to cut all ties to him. I know it will be hard. Therefore, instead of calling him Darkeros, I want you to call him Gutsyfish whenever you think of him. Again, you hold the power over him too."

I liked that idea, and for the second time today, he caught me smiling.

"Why are you being nice to me, Master?"

"Because, I like seeing you this way. Don't worry I like seeing you scream, with tears of passion running down your face, just as much. However, over the years I've learned that a happy slave works a lot harder than an unhappy one.

Now, that you've stopped crying, I think it's time for you to learn how to do your own makeup. Maxwell will talk you through it a few times.

Today, I want you to focus on everyday makeup. Tomorrow, he will come back and teach you fancy nighttime party makeup. You'll figure out real fast how important it is for you to please my needs.

I can sense you're hungry, so the faster you work on your make-up the sooner you'll be able to eat." Slowly he walked to the door.

"I've put a basket with your name on it in the refrigerator. Don't eat any food except what is in your basket. You'll also find a cabinet shelf with your name on it. If you eat another human's food without their permission, their Master can punish you.

I'll show you your room later and there's a small refrigerator in there for your snack food. When something runs low, make a note of it in the pantry. You'll see the list on the board, and it will be restocked. Do I make myself clear?"

"When did you have time to stock the fridge for me?"

He smirked, "My dear little wolf, you don't really think I went out on a hunt for you. Do you?"

"No Master, I just was confused for a moment."

"You have an hour to teach her how to do her makeup, Maxwell. I want her dressed and ready to go out. When you're finished with her, she needs to look presentable enough to be seen in high society."

"Yes, Master. Zaya will be at your side in no time."

I felt like I was an outsider to the conversation between Maxwell and Balton. One minute he was comforting me, and the next he was talking as if I weren't there.

Seven

By the time, Master took me back to Patches Motel for our check-in, there was no doubt in my mind I'd stay the entire week with him.

He gave me a taste of what being by his side would be like last night at the charity function for the policeman's' ball.

I even saw Blade with his wife dancing and having a wonderful time. Every politician made it a point to come over to my Master to socialize or talk business. Not once did he introduce me to any of these people. I had been warned to stay silent and take in everything being said around the room. He had put me on hi-protocol for the night.

After a night of dancing, he took me back to the mansion as promised. He told me he was pleased with my behavior and I would get a treat.

As promised that night he took me back to his room, tied me to a Saint Andrews Cross, teased me with his belt, used a whip on my back, and even cut into me with a knife, watched the blood drain from my arm until I thought I had was on the verge of bleeding out. He then licked my arm as he had licked my pussy the night before. I wasn't allowed to shift until I was close to passing out, but in a crazy fucked up way, I trusted him. Something I cannot say I had done with anyone else.

After he was done with me, he took me back to my room where he shackled my left ankle with an iron shackle that was lined with fur, so that my ankle wasn't harmed from pulling too hard. A long steel chain was attached to the shackle.

"This will give you enough length to get to the bathroom in my suite. You have snacks and drinks in your refrigerator."

"Master, did I not please you tonight?"

"Zaya, you did more than please me. Why? Would you like elsewise? "

"In the time since I arrived a couple of days ago, I've slept in the cage under your bed. Tonight, you are putting me in my room." I couldn't control my emotions, tiny droplets formed in the corner of my eyes.

"Zaya my beautiful girl, I have a date tonight, and I don't know if we'll go back to his place or mine. You'll be safer this way. If I left you in your cage, how would you get out to go to the bathroom?"

I hadn't thought about him not coming home and leaving me all night by myself. In a way, that scared the shit out of me.

At my surprise, he said, "Gender doesn't matter to me. People are people and everyone has holes to fuck. The point is, my dear, if we come back here, there's a chance we'll make use of you and I expect you'll be on your best behavior. You will let him dominate you if his instruction doesn't contradict mine. You have permission to block him from your mind, but he'll have access to any other part of your body."

He waited until I said. "Master, my body belongs to you to use as you wish."

"I'm, pleased with your answer. If you get cold while I'm gone, get under the blanket. No clothes of any kind are to be worn while I'm not here. You picked a few books earlier from the library on manners, protocol, and serving. I want you to start your studies as we discussed earlier. Remember I plan on testing you later in the week."

****

After reading the protocol book twice I feel fast asleep. I tried to stay awake that proved to be impossible. But my eyes grew tired and closed out the darkness.

Tethered

I was asleep when Master came home. "On your knees, Marty, while I bring us our treat," I hear him order from his bedroom.

You'll call me Master tonight not, Sir.

I understand, Master. I'll behave.

Of course, you will. I haven't punished you fully yet; you only had a taste before. I'm certain you know it will be bad if I'm forced to—you just don't know how badly.

"A few rules for the evening. You won't speak unless asked a direct question. You'll defer to Marty as Sir, and you'll remain in human form unless I change you."

"Yes, Master."

He'd brought a key and unlocked my shackle as he asked how much reading I'd managed. He was asking but I already knew he knew where I'd finished.

I told him, and when he didn't respond, I lowered my head and said, "I'm sorry if I displeased you, Master. I fell asleep while I was reading."

He touched the top of my head and ran his fingers through my hair. His stroke was gentle, soothing, comforting.

"I'm pleased with your accomplishments. It's not easy, but I have faith that you will finish your task by the end of the week. Let's get you out of this shackle. You know you could have constricted your leg to slip out of my magical shackle. You didn't shift to your wolf body, and yet you didn't attempt to escape. This pleases me greatly."

Once he freed my ankle, he pointed towards my refrigerator. "Drink a bottle of water, go to the bathroom, and freshen up. Come to us in my bedroom. Kneel in the doorway, wait until you are invited." I did as he commanded. I knew he was going to enforce hi-protocol from now until he released me.

I approached Master's doorway, knelt, and waited until I was told to come in. Master was vigorously fucking the other man's ass when I knelt. I wasn't sure if I was supposed to watch, or if I should I lower my gaze to the floor as a good slave would do.

Something though intrigued me to watch. My Master's body was beautiful to look at. His back showed lines and lines of muscle. His strong arm looked like a body builder's arm. Maybe he lifted weights in his down time. Even though I had seen his body a few times, he still looked buff.

At first, I wasn't terribly turned on at watching my Master use the other man, in a way I wished it was me who was having her ass fucked. Jealousy is something I hadn't come upon yet.

Master sensed what I was feeling. He had a way of reading my mind like no other Master had done before. He had a special gift. Master let me feel what the other man felt. I was told it was also how a vampire felt. The vampire was being held down by Master's power. No chains, cuff, or physical restraints. Pure willpower from my Master.

The young vampire enjoyed having sex with men. Even though he was playing the submissive role with Master, I could tell that he had a dominant side as well. I read his mind and found out that he had been out with Master before. Master wasn't going to be easy on him tonight. He was going to use and abuse his ass.

Someday, perhaps I'll let you top him. We'll see how the evening progresses first.

I'll be whatever you need me to be Master.

Hmm, on second thought, maybe it will be tonight. A few minutes later, I realized Master wasn't allowing the other vampire to orgasm. His moans and groans sounded throughout the room.

Eight

I pulled out of Marty's ass and dragged an armless chair to the center of the room. Just below the foot of the bed. I plopped down in the chair with my cock pointed to the ceiling.

"Marty don't think I'm through with you yet. Come sit your ass on my cock. My little she-wolf, grab the flogger from the nightstand and give it to me. Once Marty is fully seated on my cock, I want you bent over the edge of the bed. "

Marty was in pure bliss while flogging the she-wolf. Each time he let the falls hit her back, he rode me in an odd sort of way. The three of us were in our little dance of delight.

This arrangement worked out for all of us, but especially for Marty. I still wasn't about to let him come. When he got close again, I passed his orgasm to Zaya and took great pleasure in forcing her to come from the pain he was inflicting on her back.

It wasn't long that I played this game between the two of them. Zaya's back, ass, and upper thighs were a nice shade of deep red with splotchy purple bruises marking her body. Screams of agony pierced my ears; I wasn't going to last much longer. I needed to throw both to the bed and fuck them into oblivion.

My girl was entering sub-space; the only sounds out of her mouth were moans and groans. After her third orgasm, she telepathically begged me not to give her any more.

"Both of you stand and face each other, Marty, when I give the okay, you may order the girl to do whatever you wish. You'll be on your own to enforce your commands. You'll have only five minutes with her, after that time she's mine. If in that five minutes, you can get her to make you come, good for you. If she doesn't well, you'll go home with a hard on."

Zaya, you're no longer under orders to obey him. If you can overpower him mentally, you can have your own fun with him. Permission to speak at will, and unless he can enforce it, you don't have to call him, Sir."

I made a small exit to moving over to a more comfortable chair. I propped my feet up on the small footstool. "Five minutes. Start Now!'

I have the best seat in the house.

"On your knees, bitch. Suck my cock for starters." Marty was certain she'd obey his command. He showed no power in his voice. Zaya made no effort in moving or dropping to her knees. She just stood and stared at the wall behind him. He put power in his gaze before he said, "Now, bitch."

Zaya didn't move. Instead, she crossed her arm over her chest. I could sense her drawing energy from the room. She tilted her head and said, "No, Martin, I think you're the one who needs to kneel."

She had poked enough in his brain to know he hated being called Martin. I stayed out of her head for now, wanting her to do this all on her own, but I'd need to find out, later. I watched as Marty fought to stay standing, and lost as his body obeyed while his mind rebelled. I put a wall up so he couldn't telepath my thoughts.

"You're on your own, Marty."

I could tell Zaya was pleased with how he obeyed her. The smile on her face told me everything.

"Master, can you teach me to use the flogger on him?"

I shook my head. "Let's save those lessons for later. Feel free to practice on his back. A few strokes won't hurt him. The good thing about having a target like him is he'll heal."

When the five minutes were up, I was ecstatic at the outcome. Marty tried not to cry because Zaya hadn't spared him. His back and ass looked just like hers. Red and bruised. Zaya's first few hits didn't even touch him, her next few wrapped around on his chest, and even a few hit him on the tip of his dick. When she finally got the hang of swinging the flogger, she left several bloody marks on his hips and legs.

Marty was pissed and humiliated at being treated this way by the she-wolf. He tried to fight her, but she was easily holding him down. Tears seeped down his face. They were a combination of fear, frustration, and pain administered from the wolf. His cock was limp, no longer hard. As soon as she saw his wilted cock, she commanded him to make it hard again.

This vampire was a switch; he couldn't submit to someone weaker than us. It's both physically and mentally impossible. As, long as I was giving the orders, he was submitting to me.

The moment I said, "Times up," my she-wolf stopped flogging Marty. She immediately dropped to her knees as she said, "Thank you, Master."

I ran my fingers through her hair as I had done so many times before. She knew that was the sign I was pleased with her behavior. "You're welcome, sweetheart."

I had no idea.

I know. If you stay with me, I'll eventually let you use my powers with others, as well as your own. However, you should know you'll pay the price for it when we're alone. Being mine won't be easy but the rewards are tenfold.

Having a powerful wolf at my side impressed me. Somehow, most of the other vampires would fear her nearly as much as they feared me. Knowing I could control such a powerful creature, I trusted her when I was dead to the world.

I finished the evening off with Zaya bent over the bed, Marty buried in her snatch, and me filling his ass. Zaya was rewarded with another orgasm as I was.

Marty, however was sent to the upstairs bedroom frustrated. No orgasm for him. I did let him feed from her neck. Small sips were drained, just enough to wet his appetite. I let Zaya sleep in her cage under my bed. She wasn't allowed to change into her wolf form; instead, she was commanded to read more.

Nine

Master sent for the stylist again today. I figured we were going out to another fancy charity gathering. Boy was I wrong. Instead, another man arrived at the mansion. He presented a new identity to my Master. He was having me made up to look exactly like the documents.

Master quizzed me for hours about my new identity I was assuming. I had so many questions about the person identification. Before I could get my question out, Master said in a stern voice, "she was a runaway, and dead."

I looked at my Master, realize he wasn't in the mood to see my strength come to head. I dropped my gaze to signal my submission.

Master told me I'd be introduced as Zaya Phillips from now on. I loved my new name; it was much better than my birth name. Bailey Chips.

We talked at length about our scene last night with Marty. Master loved dissecting everything; he went as far as asking how I knew about Marty's nickname. This was the key factor in Marty submitting to me. I had no idea it was a trigger for Marty to be called Martin. It was a gift that I could dig that deep into his mind. I had used it before with people.

Master made sure I looked the part of being his. He had the hairdresser and stylist come back for more lessons. Along with me studying more etiquette books prepping me for my final exam in two days. Add to this the fact Master thoroughly used me every possible second he could get his hands on me. He drained me, I was running on fumes despite the fact I had an unlimited amount of red raw meats.

The day before my final night with him, he left me in wolf form after he fed from me. He took me to the basement; it was cold dark and damp. Just like basements were supposed to be. In the middle of the room was a small cage. I wasn't sure why he was punishing me like this. Had I displeased him? My job as his slave didn't give me the right to question his authority over me.

"Sleep my little wolf." None of my fancy things were in the room. "You'll be fine." He held my gaze and repeated, "You'll be fine. *Trust.*

Trust is the key to this relationship. You Zara, hold that key. Before he locked the cage, he stroked my hair one more time. Slowly I settled down. Just from his touch. I watched as he turned the lights off. I heard him in my head, ordering me to sleep. I did exactly what he commanded me to do. Sleep. Or more importantly I had to obey his command.

****

Disoriented, I woke when the lights came on. A strange person looked through the bars of the cage. I wasn't sure who he was. I read his mind and found out he too was a vampire. I quickly blocked him from reading my mind. I brought up the walls around my thoughts, just in case he tried to read mine.

"So, you're the little she-wolf keeping my second in charge busy this week." He unlocked the door, opening it and motioned me out.

I kept my ground in the cage, afraid to move.

I wondered why my Master hadn't warned me that his Lord Leigh would wake me. He did tell me that I had to trust him. I had never met Lord Leigh but had learned a lot in the past week about him from my Master.

"He didn't want to scare you last night. Knowing you would worry yourself sick. Plus, he wanted you to have a full night's sleep."

Shit, he just heard my thoughts; I thought I could block him. Was I wrong? I let down the walls when I realized his powers were much greater than mine. He was one of, if not the strongest, vampires of all time.

I did as I was commanded. I walked out of the cage and kneeled, waiting for my next directive.

"Change."

He changed me. I had forgotten that I was still in wolf form. I didn't stand as I normally did when changing to human form. I stayed kneeling at his feet. I lowered my head and gazed at his shiny shoes, and said, "My Lord Leigh."

"Yes, I am. Balton tells me you're self-aware about your body hair when you change from wolf to human. I don't want you stressing yourself. I've seen many she-wolves."

Balton could make me come back with my hair and nails the same as before I shifted. However, he refused to do anything about my body hair. I felt something was wrong with me, but in the end, I knew not to argue with my Master. That would only lead him to punishing me more.

I kept my gaze down. "Yes, Master."

"Good girl. On your feet and follow me. I keep a suite of rooms down here, and if you're going to be a part of Master Balton's house, then we need to come to our own agreement first."

I didn't know what he was talking about. "I don't have an official agreement with my Master yet, Master."

He chuckled. "You can call me My Lord Leigh for the time being. I know calling us both Master can be challenging. I don't mind you using my name if an honorific is included. I hope that in time Balton will do the same."

His suite was nicely decorated in a Victorian style everything matched perfectly. The colors on the walls were a deep red. It reminded me of a ripe tomato. The room was lush and elaborate. I could only image what his mansion was like.

He sat in a chair made for a king and motioned me to kneel in front of him. "I keep track of all those who have special powers. And you my dear, slipped under my radar. Balton seems to believe that you were unaware of your powers. You've shown me a crack in my security. One which I've taken steps to patch, but that isn't why I summoned you here today."

I glanced around the room one more time. At first, I heard the clicking of a clock but couldn't find it. It was only after I looked a little harder when I saw it was only a little after three o'clock. Balton was most likely still a sleep. He usually woke up around four p.m., which left me on my own with My Lord Leigh. I trembled with fear.

"I'm aware Balton put a temporary leash on you for the past week. I don't plan to do that today. You do need to know that Balton belongs to me first, and if I choose, I could have access to your leash at any time. Once you two make a long-term agreement you will belong to me as well."

I nodded when he paused, unsure of what kind of response he was looking for.

I heard him sigh. "I'm going to poke around in your head. I would do this whether you're with Balton or not."

"Of course, my Lord Leigh. I understand fully." I didn't resist, I made every effort to open my mind. Again, I remembered my Master's words 'trust, you hold the key.'

I knew better than to use my powers on him. So instead, I sat patiently while he took hold of my mind. Once he was done, he leaned back in his chair with a sigh.

"Balton is rough on his slaves, but he'll give you a better life than the one you ran from. If you accept his agreement, you'll be expected to be called up by me. I may want to use and abuse you, or I might want you to feed or service a guest who might grace my company. You do know that Balton intends to pamper you to the fullest. Behind closed doors he plans on using and abusing you until you can't take any more."

I dared not look him in the eyes when he talked about my future if I agreed to stay. I heard him shift out of his chair. His clothes were being shed. "Slaves have no right in the underworld. However, the few I allow to be enslaved in my territory may always come to me if they have a valid complaint against their Master. Make sure your complaint is of the highest complaints. Likewise, should any of my slaves feel they need a mediator, they're allowed to go to Balton. Make sure you truly understand my words. Now, as my temporary property, I have the right to sample your goods. Go to the foot of the bed, and bend over, showing me your ass. You'll take my belt first, and then you'll take my cock. If you please me, I will reward you by feeding from you."

Ten

I woke to her screams in my head. The sound of her being whipped brought my cock to attention. I smiled as I realized he wasn't sparing her at all. I slowly went down the steps and entered my Master's suite. Telepathically my Master let me know I should come in without knocking. I smelled blood as I entered. My girl was standing in the corner of the room, hooked to a chain embedded into the ceiling. Her wrists had been cuffed. Her toes barely touched the floor. She was marked from head to toe. She screamed until she was hoarse, tears streamed down her face.

My Lord Leigh turned to me with a smile. "Ah, Balton she is such a treat. Would you like to beat her, before we fuck her?"

I smirked, "No I think you've managed a thorough job. Did you find anything in her memories I missed?"

"No, I feel certain she poses no threat to us or our territory. I can add to your programming. So that our little she-wolf doesn't try to override the control you'll have over her will. She'll just think what I've put there are her wishes and won't realize I've installed them."

I looked forward to transforming my little she-wolf. With the help of my lord, I knew we could control her. This meant I could give her free rein in my quarters.

She'd be the best little guard, the perfect slave to obey and to teach others in time. Most of all she'll be the best supernatural at my side.

"Thank you for the offer, Master. We have much to accomplish in the short time, before the sun sets and then rises. You are my lord, which hole would you like to have? I've had all three, they're divine. Which do you prefer?"

"I've already had her ass a few times; perhaps I'll try out her pussy." He stepped to her front and used his powers to levitate her. She was still shackled to the chain hooked in the ceiling. He spread her legs, opening her up to him. He positioned her so that she could sit on his cock. Once she was fully seated on his cock, I went to the nightstand and found the lube. Her ass had been used a few times already today. She'd be most likely sore from all the abuse. I slicked up my cock prepping it to take her.

Our little she-wolf had been put under a spell by my Master. She couldn't move, scream, or moan until he released his spell on her. She was our toy to use as we wanted.

I crammed myself into her puckered ass. She didn't have time to adjust to the pain. Once I filled her, my Lord released the spell. She instantly let out a yelp then a moan. My little she-wolf was in-tuned to what was happening to her.

I looked over her shoulder at my lord and smiled. We'd shared plenty of submissives before. He knew that I was waiting for him to set the rhythm before I started pumping my cock in her ass.

My Lord was the only vampire that fucked me. It was his power over me. I was his as Zaya was mine. Mostly, we were two dominants using a bottom. Neither one of us had to hold back today. Our little she-wolf was everything to both of us now.

The smell of sex and hormones filled the room. I felt pleasure providing my wolf to my Master. The situation apparently had a similar effect on Leigh. He shared his hunger with me telepathically and we both leaned into her neck, and bit simultaneously. She tasted the best I had ever tasted from her before.

I was in her head and she knew it. I took in everything around us. Her savory blood tasted fresh going into our mouths. She gave us her powers as we sucked her dry. She held nothing back; she gave us her trust, power, and energy. She emitted her aura all around us.

She wanted to be in us, wanted to nourish us, but most of all she submitted to both of us. She was a true submissive.

We pulled out of her neck at the same time. He released her cuffs from the chain. I pulled my cock from her ass, as My Lord Leigh pulled out of her pussy. She was limp in my arms. Her arms went around my neck. I licked both sides of her neck where she'd been bitten. I sealed both holes with a numbing substance from my salvia.

I gently placed her on the bare floor. I ran my hands over her entire body, tracing the welts from my Master. She was flying high in sub-space. This was one memory I would leave for the rest of her life. Our time was flying by so fast. We had much to do, so I ordered her to change back to being a wolf.

Eleven

After going months without changing in to my super natural side, I'd made up for that this week. I couldn't count how many times my Master had commanded me to shift. I never minded shifting for him. The fluctuation in his voice both had me on a sexual high and scared to death.

Master never starved me as others had done before. I had an endless quantity of fresh red meat at my disposable. My energy level had surged, and so did my powers. In return, I gave him my trust, powers and energy. The exchange between us was amazing.

I had learned in the past week how my powers worked. I had no idea that I held such greatness. It was comforting, having control over my growth. I had only agreed to a one-week trial; our time would end at sunrise tomorrow morning. He would return me back to Patches Hotel, where Blade waited for me. In a way, I didn't want this night to end. I had learned to trust him, even if it was only for a week. I didn't know what the next ten hours held for me. I knew Blade would interrogate me once I returned.

As I shaved, fixed my hair and applied my makeup the way he loved. Master explained how the rest of the night would be like. In a way, I felt sad deep in my heart. I knew he read my mind it wasn't unusual now.

"My Lord Leigh and I will be flying to Boston to deal with some problems in that territory. I want you by my side as my companion, submissive, but most of all I want to show you off as my guard dog. I'll give you enough energy and power to bring everyone to their knees."

I wasn't sure how I felt being given my Master's power. I relished the fact he trusted me enough with such conviction. Especially since I had only been under his training for a week. A part of me thought this must be my final test. I would not disobey my Master's commands. Amazing energy emitted from my Master, I had only been to a few events this past week. He had told me that part of being second in command was keeping several territories in check. I wasn't sure what that meant. I was soon to find out.

"Master you said we would be flying, the three of us. How is that going to work since I've never flown before?" He smoothed down his hand on my head, as he had done so many times before. He used it as a calming tool.

"If we want to, we could support you between us as we fly, but we'd need to make sure safety came first. I would hate to be flying and suddenly lose you to a hawk or even worse a vulture."

I could tell by the expression on his face he was joking. That was a side to him that I loved. Yeah, he was a Sadist at times but he also had a humorous side.

"My dear, you mean more to me and Lord Leigh, it's easier to take one of his charter planes."

Once we touched down in Boston, a limo waited for the three of us. The ride from the airport to the house where we would be meeting the other vampires only took roughly ten minutes. The neighborhoods we drove through were pristine and well-manicured. The underground in which we just left didn't hold a candle to this fancy neighborhood.

Upon entering the house, Master levitated me off my feet. He flanked my right side, and Lord Leigh flanked my left. The three of us entered the great room. Several Vampires sat at a large round table. Slowly Master lowered me to the ground. He had levitated me several times during the week, each time he did it sent a thrill throughout my body. I felt like I was having tiny orgasms.

Master, telepathed me and said, "You're up my little wolf."

I knew exactly what he wanted me to do. I wasn't just representing my Master, but I was also here in capacity of My Lord Leigh's representative. The power that the two of them trusted me with was mind blowing. Never had I had this type of position.

I took a deep breath and stepped forward.

"How dare all of you. Kneel before our Lord Leigh. Show him the respect that he has earned over the last thirteen hundred years."

Every one of the vampires, five in total in the room, jumped up from their chairs. Before they could kneel on their own, I used my powers by shoving them to their knees. I used force on each one of them. I couldn't be gentle. I had to prove to them I meant business. I held the power, not them.

Looking back over the past week, hell even the last month, if someone would have told me that I could bring five powerful vampires to their knees I would have thought they were out of their minds. Let alone stand in front of the two most powerful vampires of all time, I would have laughed in their faces.

I'd stood in front of them in my wealthy socialite attire, without fear but instead with conviction. No one would ever fuck with me, if I had my Master and Lord Leigh by my side.

After business was conducted between the seven vampires, two had been killed and the other three were being banished from Lord Leigh's territory. It was no different from what Blade did back at Patches Hotel.

Twelve

On the plane ride, back to the underground, Master outlined a new contract between the three of us. My Lord Leigh would directly oversee that Master Balton would hold up to the contract. And with that contract came some pretty perks. Not only would I have my own bank account, unlimited amounts of clothes, shoes, and accessories, but also I would have servants to take care of me.

With these perks, I would be taught how to use my powers to the fullest. I would be in service to Master Balton and to Lord Leigh whenever he requested my service.

I wouldn't have access to my bank account while my slavery terms were in effect. I would only be granted use after my twenty-year contract expired, or, if I found someone I wanted to bind myself to romantically. The only caveat was he would only release me to another vampire and not to a human. I knew my Master was loaded financially; in return, he would make me a rich she-wolf when my contract was over. Something I had always dreamt about.

"Let me be clear, Zaya," he said, his eyes were dark as coal and scarier than any other time I had seen them. "You'll never be anything more to me than a slave behind closed doors, but when were out in public you will serve me. If I ever settled down with a companion, you will serve both of us. No matter if you like it or not."

He was very serious, offering me the benefits, powers, financial stability that came along with my slavery. Time seemed to stand still as he went over the fine terms of the contract. I hadn't felt the plane touchdown. Before I knew it, I was being ushered back into a limo. He told me that we would be back to the underground in ten minutes.

What I didn't expect was for all my things to be in My Lord Leigh's limo. Not only my stuffed cat I'd brought with me, but everything Master had bought for me in the past week.

"You have two days to come back to me, my little wolf. I'm closing our connection and detaching the leash, so you won't be able to telepath me. I don't want to influence your decision. You need to make this all on your own.

Blade has arranged work for you, if you decide not to take me up on my offer." He handed me an envelope, filled with the money he owed for the past week. I didn't expect him to pay me directly.

"If you don't come back to me, I'll have no hard feelings against you. Maybe I can arrange for occasional use of your service from Blade, but again, that is all up to you."

"Master, why are you sending me away like this?" Tears began to soak her cheeks.

"No, little wolf. I'm not sending you away. Our agreement was for one week."

Balton did not speak instead My Lord Leigh spoke up. "You won't contact him until after nine thirty tomorrow night, no matter your decision. The cut-off is two days from now, before sunrise. If you decide against it, and change your mind a week from now, you'll need to go through me before I'll validate your contract. You'll find in the envelope both of our numbers, just remember you need to make a clear choice."

I turned to my Master. "Did you make me forget anything about this week?"

He shook his head. He wasn't about to break his silence which made the situation worse. I watched as Master Balton got into another car and drove away.

My Lord Leigh drove me back to Patches Hotel with all my possessions. We rode in silence. Before he released me to Blade he said, "You're no longer under my protection, little wolf, and thus if you get in trouble you are not to use your powers. This is a tough decision; trust your heart to guide you in the direction it takes you. Remember you hold the key to your heart. Trust in yourself must come from you, Zaya. "

I looked around my small pathetic room, especially since Master's mansion was so huge and elaborately decorated. I had to come to grips he was no longer my Master he was just Balton to me now. In a way, I was sad. I had gotten use to calling him Master. If I didn't go back to him, I couldn't call him Balton. It just wasn't natural to me.

Balton had given me more in the past week than any other Master had ever given me. I could use everything as I wished.

After putting away some of the gifts Balton had given me. I suddenly became very tired. I fell asleep weighing all my options, without a clue of what I was going to decide. What stuck out in my head was Balton didn't command me to extend my contract. It felt almost like a business proposal. Both of them had used the word trust over and over.

Thirteen

I tossed and turned for five hours, sleeping in my bed was not as soothing as my cage back at Balton's place. I missed the secure feeling of being safe in my cage.

I had set my alarm for ten but around six am I couldn't see myself falling back to sleep. I knew that Blade never slept either, so I texted him if we could meet for lunch.

He immediately texted back, "What's up?"

"I need to bounce some questions off you."

"Are you turning down Balton's contract?"

"I don't know."

"Sweetheart, remember you can talk to me about anything. I'm the only family you have. No matter what you decide. We protect family. And that means you. Be in the parking lot at noon. I'll send one of my guards to pick you up. Remember if he doesn't give you the word of the day don't get in the car with him. You do know what the word of the day is?"

"Thirteen."

"Correct, see you soon."

I searched in my closet for casual clothing, nothing like the fancy stuff Balton bought me. Most of the ball gowns I wouldn't be able to wear for everyday clothing. Jeans and a t-shirt would do for lunch. I'd splurged with a touch of makeup.

I was sure Blade wouldn't recognize me with the new hair color, but he surprised me when he looked me up and down. I think that was the first time he took notice of me. I walked to the back of the bar, just as Blade had instructed.

"Thanks for meeting me; I really just want you to be my sounding board. I need to come to a decision and the clock is ticking away." I sighed just as I finished my sentence.

"I'm the one who has to hand you over if you decide to accept his contract. You do know that you'll be handed over to both vampires, don't you?"

"I do. Did he tell you he changed my name to Zaya and had a whole new identity made up?"

"I'm aware of the changes. I think it fits the new you. I know Balton can be a sadistic bastard and a hard ass when it comes to business, but he also has another side to him that stands out for his character. He's always up front and honest. No matter what the outcome. Ultimately the choice is yours."

"His contract is very thorough; we talked about the pros, and cons, so I know what I'll be getting myself into. It's strange how I trusted him from the moment I met him. He emits a different vibe than any other vampire I've ever been with. I know having my freedom hasn't been the best for me. I was never truly happy. My inner submissive side needs the heavy hand of a Master, especially when it comes to obeying his commands.

I yearn for this daily. I think he'll balance the good with the bad over time. Just in the short time I was with him he taught me so much about myself that I never realized I had inside of me."

Just like that, I knew I had already accepted his contract before sealing the deal. The contract wasn't just about material things, but more so about the fact he saw me for who I am. I'm more than a she-wolf to him. No one had ever seen me for who I was not even my parents or another pack member. I was just a she-wolf to them.

"I think our little she-wolf has made up her mind," Blade said.

"I guess I have, thank you for listening to me. I've always felt like I could express myself to you in a way you made me see clearly. "

"I took on that role to protect you. Remember even though you'll be signing a contract with Balton. I will make sure he holds up to everything stipulated on that piece of paper. I stand to lose just as much as you do if things go sour. I read over the contract and the only thing I find not to my liking is the length of terms. I think twenty and ten is out of the question. I would like the contract to be amended to a thirteen-year term. After you finished the last year, I want you to be able to take a month off without pressure. Then after the month is over if you want to re-oath to him I will stand by your side once again. Are you ready for me to set up the meeting between the four of us? "

Blade was looking out for me, not what he was about to gain or lose. I smiled back to him, remembering when the organization took me in as part of their family. None of Blade's partners mistreated me. I was always family to them. I would always be grateful to Blade.

Blade leaned forward and said, "Just remember who took you in when you get big and powerful. Your role will be more important than what you think. You will hold the keys to the underworld."

I couldn't finish my lunch; my stomach was in knots. Not sure if it was the excitement or being scared all at the same time. I would need to get myself under control before seeing Balton again.

"I'll see you during the contract signing," Blade told me. "And I know Balton will know everything we've told you, which is fine. If at any time, you change your mind all you need to do is speak up. I will stop everything at once. Who knows freedom might look a little different after thirteen years. You might want to take your money and move on."

Blade had no idea I didn't know if I wanted my freedom or not. I had been trapped in my body for so long I wasn't sure how to expect freedom to be.

Fourteen

I pulled out the envelope that Balton had given to me a day ago. I sent two texts, one to Balton, and one to Lord Leigh. They both replied that they would meet me at Balton's mansion as promised.

I was full of nerves and scattered thoughts. Blade accompanied me to the mansion. We were escorted to the great room. Lord Leigh and Balton, dressed in black leather, were already waiting for us. Both looked like they had just stepped out of a Boris Karloff movie set.

Candles lit up the entire room. Refreshments were carefully displayed on the three hundred year old buffet. I wasn't sure if I would be able to eat a thing without barfing it back up due to my nerves. I already felt home, it had only been twenty-four hours since I last was here. In a way, this place was cozier than my little room back at Patches Hotel.

Blade had negotiated my price earlier in the day. After several debates, back and forth between the three of them, they agreed to a Thirteen and ten-year contract. Not the twenty and Thirteen-year contract that Balton had wanted. I wasn't sure why Balton had wanted that many years with me. In a way, it made me feel special. Maybe, this was his way of taking me as his for good.

Several ceremonial rituals had to be done before signing the contract. He started out with a naming ceremony, in which Balton presented me with my new name Zaya Phillips. I was already use to being called Zaya from the week of service I had already finished. I didn't question my last name; I was just a little curious on where it came from. I had plenty of time to ask him once the contract was signed.

I felt my aura change when he called me by my new name. I didn't let my emotions take over as I had done in the past.

Balton commanded me to remove all my clothes and kneel at his feet. I did as told. My body became super sensitive as the six sets of eyes stared at my body. I had never been super conscious of what my body looked like but having it on parade was strange. I'd memorized the statement to be given as my oath.

Balton smelled my neck; he licked the sensitive artery that pumped my blood. He wrapped his arms around me, securing me in his grip. I felt his fangs pierce my skin. I was instantly his. Pain screamed throughout my body. He didn't soothe or ease the pain he was inflicting upon me. He hadn't numbed my neck at all. I had never felt this type of pain before. Not even the first time he bit me.

I opened my eyes but didn't focus on anything or anybody in the room except for my Master.

"Slave, I need to hear you proclaim your oath to everyone in the room."

"I, Zaya Phillips, do hereby oath my mind, body, spirit, will and soul to Master Balton, second in command to My Lord Leigh, for a maximum period of thirteen years or if deemed appropriate no less than a ten-year term."

I felt him command me to shift from human to wolf. His fangs were still piercing my neck.

Yours, we're yours. Everything. Yours.

My Lord Leigh walked towards us. He bit my Master's arm and held it to my mouth. I had fed on his arm several times in the past, today though his blood was sweeter, richer, and pure. I savored the moment.

"Change now." My Master commanded and so, I did. From wolf, back to human. My energy level had been surged just from his blood. My Lord Leigh bit his forearm and held it to my mouth; I lapped at the blood like a starving dog. Slowly I felt my Master pull out from my neck. He licked the wound closed, turning me over to My Lord Leigh, he also sealed the puncture wound in my neck. The three of us were sealed together. My contract had been signed in blood.

"Who are you now?"

"I'm your slave, property to do as you command." My Lord Leigh took my hand and placed it under my Master's and his on top of ours, he said, "So be it. This bond can't be broken without my blessing. Both of you are in my service."

I felt my Master wrap his leash around me. I had longed for that feeling ever since he took it off me twenty-four hours ago; this was the bond I lived for. No longer was I alone. Master had woven his intentions into my mind. I leaned against him, drunk on his blood. Relieved I no longer needed to be on my own. I no longer needed to make decisions on my own.

You'll make the decisions I want you to make. You're mine to do with as I wish.

I love it when you're in my head, Master. I've missed this feeling. Thank you, Master.

He smiled as if indulging me. *Why are you thanking me, my little she-wolf?*

For making me yours. For seeing who I can be, and for wanting to teach me how to use my powers. No one has ever cared about me that much before. I'm blessed.

I felt him in my head, probing. I realized he was making sure I wasn't fantasizing about him loving me. I knew that he would never love me as husband or wives do. Just having him see the truth of it, I was grateful, humbled in a way.

Maybe, just maybe over time his feelings would change to something else. And with the help from my Lord Leigh, he could urge a union between us. For that to happen, I had thirteen years to convince him.

Other books by Abigail

Bound by her Master: Book 1 in The Heart Series.

Sophie Spencer is a happily married, twenty-nine year old cardiologist. Suddenly her world is shattered to pieces. The love of her life, her only love, is taken from her in a devastating car accident. Stricken with grief, depression, and loneliness for the past two years, Sophie takes the advice of a close friend to venture down a new path – exploring the inner sides of submission. Not knowing what it truly means to submit, Sophie indulges her desires by visiting a prominent BDSM club on her own. Could she fully submit to another man's will, or was the bond that she shared with her husband unbreakable? That's the question Sophie must come to terms with.

Kyle Zeller is one hundred percent Alpha male. He owns a high end BDSM club, but has not been in a serious relationship for over a year. Serious skeletons that are buried deep in the back of Kyle's mind keeps holding him back from making a true commitment, which is until Sophie Spencer walks into the Cellar. Kyle see's for the first time in his life the person he's been looking for, she standing in front of him. He already knows everything about Sophie's past, including her desires to submit. Will Kyle's past resurface and shatter this potential relationship too?

Second Chances: Book 2 in the Heart Series

Knowing that happily-ever-afters only happen in fairy tales, Sophie Spencer spends an amazing night with her Prince Charming. Being new to the lifestyle, she allows her hidden fears to take over and does the unthinkable. She screams her safe-word…and runs directly into danger. Will her moment of weakness cause her world to be torn apart again? Or will she overcome her trust issues and fully surrender to her Prince.

Falling in love had been the furthest thing from Kyle Zellar's mind, but when Sophie Spencer fully submits to his dominant demands, his only recourse is to claim her as his. Before he can claim her, he is forced to let her go.

Fighting his inner demons and past issues of childhood abandonment, he knows he must sort out his own life before he can move on with his future.

But will it be too little too late?

Taming His Submissive: Book 3 in the Heart Series

Author's note: This is the third book in The Heart Series, and NOT a standalone. You, of course, can read them in any order you like, but I would recommend you read Bound By Her Master first and then Second Chances.

Theirs To Love: Book 1 Doms of Crave County

One curvy, redheaded attorney; two sexy twins. Sometimes you must face your demons head on... Determined to forget a dark secret in her past, Charlotte Maxwell left home when she turned eighteen, immersed herself in textbooks, and eventually launched a successful career as a prominent New York attorney. Isolating herself from family, friends and co-workers, she allows depression, fear, and most of all sexual tension to build up inside her, mind, body, and soul.

Eight years later, she's forced to return to her hometown of Crave County, where everyone lives some sort of kinky lifestyle, her parents being amongst the many. Tasked with adjudicating her parents' estate after their unfortunate deaths, Charlotte's hidden demons begin to resurface and along with her attraction for two of the hottest businessmen ever to steam up a room.

Mackenzie and Dillon Ryder were born and raised in Crave County. Practicing what the town preaches has always been a part of who they are. Despite their mutual cravings for the feisty redhead, they have always considered Charlotte Maxwell off limits. These two sexual dominates have been searching for their missing puzzle piece since high school. No submissive has come close to completing their circle, not until Charlotte needs them to rescue her. Not only is she the answer they've been looking for, but she too has been secretly pining for them. Will fate bring these three together, or will their insecurities separate them for good?

Ours To Love: Book 2 Doms of Crave County

One curvy, blonde waitress; One sexy chef; One hot restaurant manager. Together they make a recipe for love!

Gloria Jean Fitzpatrick carries a dark horse not only etched within her mind, but branded on her skin as a permanent reminder of the abuse she has suffered. After ending a three year long abusive D/s relationship, she believes her days of submission are over.

Heart broken, wounded, and alone, she devotes her waking hours to taking care of her disabled brother, working crazy shifts at the local diner, and over indulging in life's finest pleasures, sweets.

Carefully guarding her heart, Gloria watches as her two closest male friends continue to dominate other submissives. Dreaming of much more than friendship, she makes the hardest decision of her life, but will her hidden demons hold her back?

Greg and Curtis O'Malley are no strangers to the art of domination and have been dominating willing submissives together for years. Life for these two sexy cousins has surely had its ups and downs. Dishing up savory meals at Maxwell Diner is only one of Greg O'Malley special gifts, his other… dominating a willing submissive.

Escaping the big city to manage Maxwell Diner was a life changing move for Curtis O'Malley. Now his quest to find the perfect submissive to complete his and George's nexus may finally be over, but will Gloria's past come back to haunt their happiness?

The Doms of Crave County series contains mature themes including heart pounding action, suspense, graphic violence, and a lot of steamy hot sex with multiple partners.

Lucky 13: Volumes 1 and 2

Quickies, a perfect indulgence when stuck waiting in line, relaxing before bed, or for a quick fix during your lunch break. Step into the pages with seven short reads sure to wet your appetite and stir your imagination. These sexy Doms will take your mind on an erotic journey and arouse your deepest desires where all things are possible within the dark corners of our mind where fantasies take shape for our own pleasure.

About the Author

Abigail Lee Justice writes emotional, erotic, romantic suspense that includes a BDSM theme. She creates strong characters who seem real but are flawed in some ways; some couples Happily Ever After will be a work in process. Some characters' problems are just too steamy to fix in one book.

Born and raised in Baltimore City by two wonderful, supportive, loving parents, as a child Abigail made up vivid tales in her head. Until one day, a friend told her instead of keeping her stories locked her head she needed to put them on paper and that's exactly what she did.

Abigail met her husband thirty years ago on a blind date (thanks Dan C.) while working a part time job to put herself through college. She fell madly in love with her Prince Charming and has been since the first day they met.

By day, Abigail practices medicine in a busy Cardiologist practice. By evening, she switches her white coat for more relaxed comfortable clothing.

She has two wonderful adult sons and a very spoiled chocolate lab. In the wee hours of the night, she writes BDSM romances. In her spare time when not working or writing, Abigail enjoys reading, concocting vegetarian dishes, scuba diving, high adventure activities, living in the lifestyles she writes about, and doing lots and lots of research making sure her characters get it just right. If you'd like to become part of Abigail's street team or become a beta reader for future books, drop her a message on FB@ abigailleejustice or visit her website @ www.abigailleejustice.com

Made in the USA
Columbia, SC
14 February 2020